Hi, Reader!

You're about to meet the amazing kids in Mrs. Z's third-grade class at Curiosity Academy.

Throughout the series (and the school year!), you'll meet students who each have a secret of their own. As you discover their stories, you'll get to know their greatest fears, their most embarrassing moments, and the quiet hopes they carry in their hearts.

From hilarious talent show disasters and recess dilemmas to math quizzes and schoolyard secrets, the kids in Mrs. Z's class are full of honesty, energy, and hilarious hijinks. You can read the books in any order; just be sure you don't miss any, because you're going to love getting to know all the students!

Curiously yours,
Kate Messner

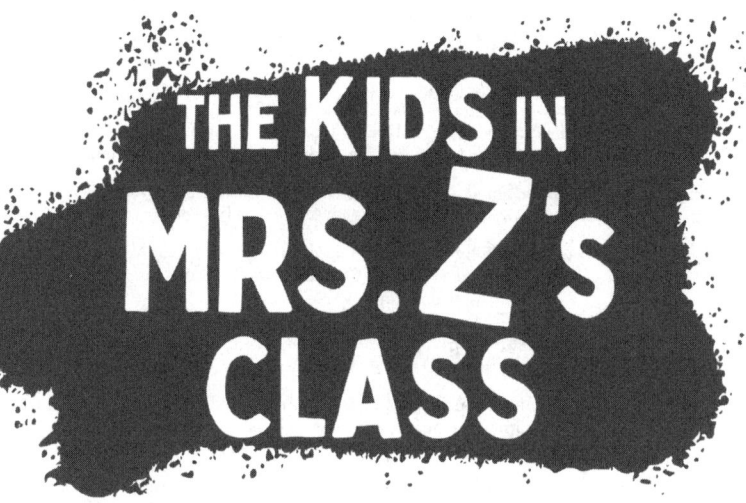

THE KIDS IN MRS. Z'S CLASS

SYNCLAIRE FIELDS KNOWS THE SCORE

BY OLUGBEMISOLA RHUDAY-PERKOVICH

illustrated by **KAT FAJARDO**

Series coordinated by Kate Messner

LITTLE, BROWN AND COMPANY
New York Boston

This book is a work of fiction. Names, characters, places, and incidents are the product of the author's imagination or are used fictitiously. Any resemblance to actual events, locales, or persons, living or dead, is coincidental.

Text copyright © 2025 by Olugbemisola Rhuday-Perkovich
Illustrations copyright © 2025 by Kat Fajardo

Cover art copyright © 2025 by Kat Fajardo. Cover design by Elena Aguirre Uranga.
Cover copyright © 2025 by Hachette Book Group, Inc.
Interior design by Neil Swaab.
Cover art color and interior shading © 2025 by Pablo A. Castro
Kraft paper texture copyright © 2025 by klyaksun/Shutterstock.com
Logo shape © doabunda/Shutterstock.com

Hachette Book Group supports the right to free expression and the value of copyright. The purpose of copyright is to encourage writers and artists to produce the creative works that enrich our culture.

The scanning, uploading, and distribution of this book without permission is a theft of the author's intellectual property. If you would like permission to use material from the book (other than for review purposes), please contact permissions@hbgusa.com. Thank you for your support of the author's rights.

Little, Brown and Company
Hachette Book Group
1290 Avenue of the Americas, New York, NY 10104
Visit us at LBYR.com

First Edition: July 2025

Little, Brown and Company is a division of Hachette Book Group, Inc. The Little, Brown name and logo are registered trademarks of Hachette Book Group, Inc.

The publisher is not responsible for websites
(or their content) that are not owned by the publisher.

Little, Brown and Company books may be purchased in bulk for business, educational, or promotional use. For information, please contact your local bookseller or the Hachette Book Group Special Markets Department at special.markets@hbgusa.com.

Library of Congress Cataloging-in-Publication Data is available.

ISBNs: 978-1-5235-3033-5 (hardcover), 978-1-5235-3032-8 (trade paperback), 978-1-5235-3034-2 (ebook)

Printed in Indiana, USA

LSC-C

Printing 1, 2025

*To my parents, who always encouraged me to try,
and to the memory of Madeleine L'Engle, who
reminded me to get over myself and get on with it*

CHAPTER ONE
100% MATH KID

"Momma, Daddy, you have twenty-seven minutes to get to the store," said Synclaire as her father handed her a banana-raspberry smoothie in the hall outside the kitchen. *Oops.* This was the third time in five days that she'd forgotten to say *Mom* and *Dad* like a big kid, instead of *Momma* and *Daddy*. She knew that three out of five was three-fifths, which was a little more than half the time. Which was too much.

"But that's okay, because today I'll have ten out of ten perfect math quizzes, which is one hundred percent, which is PERFECT!" Synclaire said, doing a little dance. Mrs. Z always gave Synclaire's perfect scores back with a quick little wink and a big smile.

"Huh?" asked her mother as Nana slipped by to turn off the whistling teakettle. "And sit down at the table to drink your breakfast, please."

"Oh, nothing. I was just talking to myself. I did the first part in my head, like a math problem," said Synclaire.

Her mother smiled, because Synclaire did that a lot. All of the Fields family did. The night before, Nana had marched up the steps muttering, "And *that's* why that dress needs the ribbon!" and none of them had even blinked.

Nana said, "So, you get your tenth math quiz back today, honey bunny?" She walked Synclaire and her friend Mars to school every day, so she had heard all about the math quizzes.

As Synclaire nodded and slid into her seat at the kitchen table, Nana poured cups of ginger tea for everyone. "There's always time for a nice cup of tea," Nana said.

Synclaire looked at the clock again. "Seven fifteen!" she said. "We have...one hour, or sixty minutes, before we need to be at school, Nana."

Daddy (whoops, *Dad*) dapped her up. "There goes our little number queen, our Number Onecher Number Cruncher!" he said.

Synclaire grinned. She loved that nickname,

even though she knew "Onecher" wasn't a real word. Synclaire's family owned a corner store in the neighborhood, and when Synclaire was there after school, she played "Beat the Cash Register" and added up the cost of people's items before her parents could finish ringing them up. Ms. Prittypat had told her that she made sure to do her shopping when Synclaire was there, "Just so I can see you work those numbers, girl. Whew! So fast! You've got something special!"

Math was who Synclaire was. Last month, her mom had given her a neon-pink T-shirt that said 100% MATH KID, and Synclaire wore it at least twice a week.

The doorbell rang. "That must be Mars!" said Synclaire, scrambling up to greet her best friend. Her mother opened the door to Mars and his mom.

"I'm almost ready, but I have to finish breakfast," Synclaire told Mars. "I want to get to school early since today's a special day!"

"Oh yeah, you remembered! Terror Time for the Dread Heads!" Mars ran an online club called the Dread Heads. From what Synclaire could see, they just talked about horror movies and played video games with lots of monsters in them.

"Uh...yeah," Synclaire said. "Terror Time. *And* we get our math quizzes back! Want to come eat?"

"Naw, I'll stay here so I can keep my shoes on," said Mars.

Synclaire gave Mars a double thumbs-up, then raced to the kitchen, where Nana had already poured her remaining tea into a travel cup. "We'll leave now, and you can sip this while we walk," said Nana. "I know you're in a hurry to get to school for your quiz results."

"Can we go to the bakery after school to celebrate ten perfect scores?" asked Synclaire, hugging her grandmother.

"We can go to the bakery because you're my granddaughter," Nana said, hugging her back. "And that's plenty enough reason to celebrate!"

The wind blew a little harder than usual as Synclaire, Mars, and Nana walked. No snow when it was this cold and windy was really NO FAIR. Nana kept checking that Synclaire and Mars had their hats pulled all the way down and their collars all the way up. "I think we're finally going to see some real snow!" she said. Synclaire was skeptical; she had counted 673 days since they'd gotten more than a light dusting.

Mars was full of stories about his latest video-game triumph. "I wasn't sure I could do it," he was saying, "and I used all my gold coins to take the 'Fear and Trembling' route across the Raging River, but—"

"Wait," Synclaire interrupted, pulling her hood even tighter around her face to block out the cold wind. "What happens if you don't make it across the river?"

"Synclaire, don't interrupt," Nana said. Then she nudged Mars. "So, what happens?"

"Oh, you fall into the ravine and it's *Game Over*," said Mars. "That happens to me all the time when I play *SuperMegaFrightFest*."

Synclaire's eyes got wide. "Like, how many times?"

"I don't know. The last three times I played,

I fell into the ravine, and I got a penalty once, too."

"Isn't there a safe way across that lets you keep your points? Just do that!" Synclaire said.

"Where's the fun in that?" said Mars. "I'm a man of action. Besides, I don't mind starting over. I don't even keep track of my points. I just like playing and trying different strategies. Here, check it out." He pointed his handheld game in Synclaire's direction, and as he did, the game made a *womp womp womp* sound. Then they all heard a big splash.

"Sounds like you didn't make it across," said Nana.

Mars shrugged. "You want to try it?" he asked Synclaire.

Synclaire shook her head. "No, thanks." Mars was really good at *SuperMegaFrightFest*, so if *he* didn't get a perfect score one hundred percent of the time, there was no way Synclaire would. Nope, she would just stick to the things that she did right already.

"Earth to Synclaire," said Mars. "I forgot to ask you about the homework. I skipped the last problem on the math worksheet. Can you explain it to me?"

"Oh no!" said Synclaire. "We're almost at school! I can explain it, but you won't have enough time to write down the answer before it's time to turn it in! It'll be like a wrong answer!"

Mars shrugged again. "I don't mind leaving it blank. I just want to make sure I know what I'm supposed to do next time."

Synclaire was silent. At school, as they settled at their tables, she wondered how Mars could be so casual about math. With ten problems on the sheet, leaving one blank automatically meant that the highest score Mars could get would be...ninety percent! Anything less than perfect was a big *womp womp womp SPLASH!* in her book. And those were sounds Synclaire did not *ever* want to hear. But she didn't have to worry about that, because her papers were always perf—

TWO WRONG?!!!

CHAPTER TWO
TWO WRONG

The marks that Mrs. Z had made on her quiz seemed to grow larger the longer Synclaire stared at her paper. She'd never noticed how angry red pen marks looked.

"I'm surprised, Synclaire," murmured Mrs. Z. She patted Synclaire's shoulder, moving on to the next table. No little smile, and no big wink!

Synclaire's throat filled up with so much air that it was hard for her to swallow.

"Are you okay?" whispered Olive.

Synclaire didn't answer. She shoved the paper into her backpack and tried to smile. "Sure!" she said. "Everything's perfect!" She looked at Olive's knitting under her desk. "What are you making?" she asked, to change the subject.

"A hat," said Olive. "Only the pattern is for babies, and I want to make it for my uncle Roy. What should I do? My uncle's head is kind of big."

"She's not lying," loud-whispered Thunder from a few tables away. "I've seen it. His head is TREMENDOUS!"

"You should increase the number of stitches to match your uncle's head," Synclaire started. Then she thought about those red marks. How could she keep giving math tips with *two wrong*? She swallowed and shrugged. "I don't know," she said.

"But you always—" started Poppy as Mrs. Z waved at their table. The week before, Synclaire had helped Poppy figure out how to triple a cupcake recipe so that they could bake enough cupcakes for the entire third grade.

"Remember, everyone, you can turn in your quiz corrections by the end of the week for full credit," said Mrs. Z. "And if you have any questions, don't hesitate to ask."

Synclaire clamped her lips shut tight. She helped *other* kids with their corrections—she didn't have to *do* them herself.

Mrs. Z went on. "Did everyone see the Daily Scribble?" she asked, pointing to the board in front of the classroom.

The Daily Scribble
for Tuesday, December 17:

what do you want to know more about?

Avoiding Poppy's worried eyes, Synclaire looked at her notebook. She couldn't write her *real* thoughts. *Why did I get two wrong on my quiz? What percent Math Kid am I now?* She wanted to know how she had suddenly stopped being the person she'd always been: the Number Onecher Number Cruncher! What if her parents found out? Or Nana? She would lose her unofficial official job at the store! Mrs. Z had said she was surprised. What if everyone at school found out? No one would ask her for help with math. Maybe they'd all stop talking to her!

Synclaire closed her notebook, shoved it in her desk, and then put her head down.

Mrs. Z came over and gently touched her shoulder. "Synclaire, do you need the nurse?"

"I can take her," volunteered Lucy. She was always going to the nurse.

Synclaire sat up and shook her head. "I'm okay," she said. "Just thinking about what to write."

Mrs. Z nodded and patted her shoulder again. "By the way, I'm looking forward to hearing from you at the next Math Club meeting. You mentioned some activity ideas for us."

Synclaire scrunched up her face. "I think you should get somebody else to do it. May I get a drink of water?" She stood up and walked away before Mrs. Z could even answer.

CHAPTER THREE
NOTHING TO CELEBRATE

Synclaire never forgot things! And she was never late! But she lost a lot of time at lunch because she was so distracted that she arrived at the cafeteria without her lunch box. So then she (1) went back to the classroom to get her lunch, and then (2) went back again for her coat for recess, and then (3) went for her hat, and then (4) went back for her lunch box *again* because she'd carried it with her to get her hat! By the time she sat down, lunch was almost over.

Synclaire sighed. Maybe aliens had taken over her body. Or maybe the aliens had snuck into Mrs. Z's class and messed with her math quiz answers. She would just focus on eating her still-warm spaghetti and meatballs.

"Your lunch smells really good, Synclaire," said Fia, who had saved Synclaire a seat while she'd been forgetting things.

"Thank you," Synclaire said, trying to smile. Mars slid over to join them.

"After we go to the bakery today, can we do homework at the store?" he asked. "We can zoom through it, and then I can show you how to play *SuperMegaFrightFest*!"

The bakery! How could she get a treat now when she had nothing to celebrate? "I don't want to go to the bakery anymore," Synclaire snapped. "And I already told you, I don't want to play that game."

"Ohhhhhkay," said Mars.

Synclaire looked up. "I'm sorry, Mars. I just...don't feel good today."

Poppy's eyes filled with concern as she leaned across the table. "You don't seem like yourself."

I'm not, thought Synclaire. *Not anymore.* If she wasn't the Math Kid, who could she be? Poppy was the Baking Kid. Olive was the Craft Kid. Mars was the Video Game Kid. Synclaire was going to have to figure out a new self, fast. She had her piano lesson coming up. Maybe she could be the Piano Kid?

"I can finish your lunch if you want," said Mars, poking her in the side and reaching for her clementine. She shrugged and let him grab it as he turned to talk to Theo about the Dread Heads. It seemed like everyone else was buzzing about the quiz.

"This one was easy!" Ruthie was practically shouting. "The easiest one yet!"

Who asked you, Ruthie? thought Synclaire, scowling. Did Ruthie even *care* about math?

"I got one wrong on the math quiz because I didn't finish the last word problem in time," Fia was saying. "I'm glad I can do it for homework."

Only *one* wrong? Synclaire almost put her head in her spaghetti container.

The lunchroom monitor shooed them all outside for recess. Synclaire, Mars, and Fia walked around the edge of the yard, avoiding the baby areas like the mini jungle gym and the unfairly off-limits fifth-grade hangout spot behind the basketball hoop.

"Are we really not going to the bakery after school, Synclaire?" asked Mars while they walked. "I was planning on a chocolate cupcake, and then I was going to get potato chips from your store, crush them up, and sprinkle them on top! I had it all worked out."

"That sounds like an interesting snack," said Fia. "And an interesting store."

Synclaire kicked at a patch of grass. "We can go to the bakery if you want to, Mars." Mars didn't have to suffer just because she wasn't a Math Kid anymore.

Fia picked up a jump rope. "Can you count for me, Synclaire? I think I'm going to hit a hundred jumps soon," she said. "Maybe today!"

Fia had been working on her jump-rope skills since Halloween. Synclaire would never tell Fia, but it hadn't looked too good in the beginning, when Fia kept tripping over the rope. On November 3, she'd only gotten to fifteen. But Fia kept trying. Most recesses, Synclaire counted while Fia jumped, faster and faster. The last time she'd made it all the way to eighty-seven.

And now Fia was probably going to take her place as the Math Kid! Synclaire bit her lip. "Are you sure you want to practice now? So many kids will be watching. What if something happens and you don't get as many as you got yesterday and everyone sees?"

"That would be kind of like traveling back in time!" said Mars, shrugging. "Which would be pretty cool."

Fia looked down. "Maybe you're right, Synclaire," she said softly.

Now Fia *looked* the way Synclaire *felt*.

"I mean, you're really good," said Synclaire quickly. "I'm just saying maybe you don't need to practice today!"

"Fia, you should come to the store after school with us," said Mars. "Synclaire has a bunch of tricks for doing math fast. She can help you with your correction and then we can all play *SuperMegaFrightFest!*" He turned to Synclaire. "Wouldn't that be fun?"

"I'm not a Math Kid anymore," said Synclaire. "And I didn't get permission to invite more friends to the store, so you can't come with us, Fia." She tried to smile so it didn't sound too mean, but it was hard to make her face look happy. "Sorry."

"That's okay," said Fia slowly. "I would have to ask permission as well."

"Look!" said Mars, showing Synclaire his game console. "The expression on your face is just like Ragin' Revenger, the Robot Avenger!" He laughed, waiting for Synclaire to join in as usual, but she didn't. "Tough crowd," he said, raising one eyebrow, which was a thing he'd

just learned how to do but was already really good at.

Coach Kayla, who was walking by, waved at Mars to put the game away. She was smiling, though, so they all knew he wasn't in real trouble.

Synclaire sighed. One-Wrong Fia was about to hit a hundred jumps and Video Game King Mars could raise one eyebrow. She was going to have to find a new thing, and fast, before she was just nobody at all.

CHAPTER FOUR
NO MORE MATH KID

At dismissal, Synclaire went over to Mars by the cubbies. As she struggled into her puffy jacket and gloves, she said, "Let's not talk to Nana about the quiz when she picks us up."

"Cool," said Mars. "I got other things to talk about, like how 'smaragdine' is a real word! I learned it last night."

"Even if she asks," said Synclaire, giving Mars a hard look. "Just...change the subject!"

Mars looked back at her with questions in his eyes, but then he shrugged. "Okay," he said. "Smaragdine means emerald green, in case you were wondering."

Synclaire looked down. "And I mean it. We can go to the bakery if you want," she murmured.

"Nah, I'm good."

Synclaire looked around the room until she spotted Fia, who was putting on a sweater, a hoodie, and a puffy jacket.

"I really like that jacket, Fia," Synclaire called out. "See you tomorrow!" She hoped that Fia understood that she was really saying, *"I like being friends with you even though I'm sorry it didn't sound like it at lunch."*

"Thanks, Synclaire," Fia said. "See you tomorrow." She smiled and waved, so maybe everything was okay.

"How was school?" asked Nana, the way she always did when she picked up Synclaire and Mars. "Ready to celebrate?" She smiled.

Synclaire tried to smile back. "Actually, we want to go straight to the store...We can go to the bakery another day. Come on, Mars!" She started to run, pulling her friend along. She glanced back to see Nana frown but start walking. Whew!

"You owe me a cupcake," whispered Mars.

"Hi, honey!" Synclaire's mom waved from a stepladder as they stepped into Fields's General Store. She was putting boxes of cereal on a top shelf.

"Just in time, Synclaire!" said their neighbor Mr. Giraud. "I'm going to make two twelve-egg omelets today. How many cartons should I buy?"

"Two," said Synclaire before she remembered that she wasn't a Math Kid anymore. But it would be rude not to finish her answer. "Because that's twenty-four eggs, and there are twelve eggs in each carton," she mumbled to the well-worn wood floor.

"Yeah!" Mr. Giraud held up a hand for a high five. Mars had to nudge Synclaire to look up and high-five back.

"Hey, hey, what's up?" Mr. Fields said to Synclaire. "Looks like it was a long day for my Number Onecher—"

"Don't call me that!" said Synclaire in a louder voice than she meant to use. "I mean...I want to come up with a new nickname." She looked from her mom to her dad. "Okay?"

Mars stared at Synclaire. "But—"

Synclaire interrupted quickly, "Can Fia come to the store tomorrow?"

"Uh...I'm sure that's fine, honey. We'll just have to meet Fia's adults first," Synclaire's mom said. "But...is everything okay? You love that nickname."

Synclaire nodded hard and focused on a spot just above her mother's head. "Yep, it's fine...I just don't want to talk about numbers so much. No biggie." She swallowed. "I like lots of things. Like...piano! And, uh... snacks..."

Nana looked at Synclaire for a moment, then clapped her hands and smiled. "That's right! So, Synclaire, why don't you and Mars go in the back, do your homework, then come back out and help me with stocking the shelves? We have a bunch of new snacks." She ushered them forward. "And, of course, there are snacks back there for you all, too. Don't spoil your dinner."

In the small stockroom, Mars and Synclaire sat down at the table. After they took out their copies of *Little Sarai, Private Eye* to do some independent reading, Mars cleared his throat.

"What's going on, for real?" he asked. "I'm not Little Sarai, but you were really happy today until we got our math quizzes back. Therefore, I deduce that something happened with your math quiz!" He looked very proud of himself.

Synclaire sighed. "It's a disaster," she said slowly. "I got TWO WRONG!"

Mars kept looking proud. "Did you like

how I did that? Maybe I should write my own detective series. Big Mars!"

"Did you even hear what I said? I got TWO WRONG on the math quiz!"

"Oh, yeah, okay. So you'll do your corrections and then we can go see what the new chips are. Maybe we'll need to taste test them, too! Oh—before I forget, can you show me your division trick again? You do it so fast!"

Mars didn't seem to understand how serious this was. "But—"

Mr. Fields peeked into the stockroom. "I hear a lot of chitchat happening. Is there a talking assignment? I can help with that! Blahblahblahdeblahbleeblahblay!"

Mars laughed, but Synclaire put her head in her hands. Parents.

Synclaire's dad held up his phone. "Mars,

your mother's on the phone. She wants to talk to you."

Mars took the phone and went out of the room. Mr. Fields sat down next to Synclaire. "So...how's it going?"

"Okay," Synclaire said. "Do you want to make up a new nickname for me?"

Mr. Fields tossed a few goldfish-shaped crackers into his mouth. "Mmmm, you know it's okay to have multiple nicknames, right? Since you mentioned piano, you can be my"—he whispered from behind his hand—"Number Onecher Number Cruncher *and* my Positively Perfect Piano Kid! See what I did there?"

Synclaire shook her head. "No more numbers."

Her father was silent for a moment, then he took a deep breath. "Synclaire, I think—"

Mars came back into the room, and Mr. Fields gave Synclaire a little hug. "We'll chat some more at home, okay?"

After her dad left the room, Synclaire closed her book. She had still been a Math Kid *yesterday*, so she could help Mars with *yesterday's* homework. "Ready for me to show you my division trick?" she said.

"Uh, that's okay," Mars said quickly. "Thanks anyway. Let's, uh, just work on our own, and then we can go help Nana." He took out his notebook and started writing immediately.

Synclaire stared at her friend for a moment, then took out her notebook, too. *He doesn't want my help anymore because I'm a math failure now!* She squeezed her eyes tight so tears wouldn't fall out. She definitely didn't want to be the Crying Kid.

It was hard not to replay the whole bad day in her mind, and she kept pausing on the expression on Fia's face when she'd said Fia couldn't come to the store. Synclaire carefully tore a sheet of paper from her notebook and wrote *INVITATION TO FIA* in big, fancy letters on one side. On the other side, she wrote:

SYNCLAIRE FIELDS REQUESTS THE
PLEASURE OF YOUR PRESENCE
AT FIELDS'S GENERAL STORE.
YOU ARE VERY WELCOME AT FIELDS'S!

She decorated the note with flowers and bees and lots of smiley faces. She'd give it to Fia tomorrow.

After homework, Synclaire and Mars helped Nana stock the shelves. Synclaire focused on the bags' colors so that she could pass them to Mars in a specific order.

"What are you doing?" asked Mars as she handed him a purple bag of Burnin' Hot Krunchy Cheesies after a lavender bag of Choco Chompers. "These are waaaaay different flavors."

"But the bags are in the same color family. Lots of people remember the stuff they buy here by how it looks. We could even make a rainbow," Synclaire said. "See, we have blues here, then it'll go from blues to purples."

"Ooh, that'll help me remember where to find Choco Chompers," said Poppy's mom, Mrs. Song, who was placing her items on the counter next to the register. "They're my secret treat. Synclaire, I'm checking out. Aren't you coming over to show this computer a thing or two?"

"I don't do that anymore," said Synclaire quickly. Then she added, "I'm sorry," in case she sounded like she was disrespecting an elder. But Nana just patted her on the shoulder.

Mrs. Song chatted with Mrs. Fields for a few minutes, then she left.

After Synclaire and Mars had finished rearranging the chips, Nana suggested they go to the bakery.

"Yeah!" shouted Mars, just as Synclaire said, "But—"

Nana held up her hand. "For some hot chocolate with lots of whipped cream. Just because, okay?"

"It's like an upside-down day," added Mrs. Fields. "You'll have dessert on your way home. Mars, your parents said it was okay, in case you were wondering."

"I wasn't, but great!" Mars grinned. "I'll go get our stuff. Synclaire, you can test me on Spelling Bee words on the way." He raced back to the storage room.

"Oh, I spoke to Fia's mom!" said Momma.

"We'll all get acquainted tomorrow after school," said Nana. "Fia will walk here with us, and her mom will pick her up from the store."

"Fia's family lives very close to us!" said Momma. "I'm surprised we haven't met them already."

Synclaire sighed. She was tired of people being surprised.

"I feel a group hug coming on," said Momma, and Nana nodded. Synclaire let herself sink into their arms.

CHAPTER FIVE
GETTING TO CARNEGIE HALL

After a comforting mug of hot chocolate and then stew peas with dumplings for dinner, Synclaire's stomach was very full, and her eyes were heavy. But she had to practice piano, because if she was going to be the Piano Kid, she was going to have to be even more serious about playing all the right notes. Maybe she'd even play during Sharing Time in music class this week! She put on her long dress from her last birthday party and sat up straight on the piano bench. She wiggled her fingers and held her hands up the way she'd seen a fancy pianist do it at Carnegie Hall in New York City.

"Why are you all dressed up?" asked Momma, walking into the living room.

"I'm preparing for my music class recital," said Synclaire. "And then Carnegie Hall."

"Happy practicing," said her mother, smiling, "and please don't mess up your clothes."

Synclaire smiled and nodded. She'd been working on this new piece, *Snowflake*, for a while.

Dahhhh duh dah dahhhh dahdahdahdah *PLUNK—*

Oops! She started again.

Dahhhh duh dah dahhhh dahdahdahdah *PLUNK—*

Ughhhhh!

Dahhhh duh dah dahhhh dahdahdahdah
PLUNK—

Dahhhh duh dah dahhhh dahdahdahdah
PLUNK—

Dahhhh duh dah dahhhh dahdahdahdah
PLUNK—

Argh! Maybe she needed to play faster.
PLUNKPLUNKPLUNK!

Her hands crashed down on the keys. Her piano teacher, Mrs. Dwyer, had told her that people who were good at math were often great musicians, too. Maybe now that she was bad at math, she couldn't play the piano anymore!

Mr. Fields peeked into the living room. "Was that a new part of the song?" he asked quietly. "It sounds...emphatic."

"What does that mean?" asked Synclaire.

"It's like you want to call a little extra

attention to something," he said, sliding onto the bench next to her.

"Oh," she said. "No, I was just...playing. Sorry if it was a little loud." She pointed to the apron he wore over his tracksuit. "What are you making?"

"I'm helping your mother with her world-famous chocolate crackers," he answered. "We've got some tasty days of dessert ahead!"

"Maybe I can help, too, after I finish piano practice," said Synclaire. And maybe she'd get an early sample—suddenly her stomach had room again.

"Maybe. You've got to get ready for bed soon—and did you finish all your homework? I heard Mars telling his mother he had some vocabulary work to get done."

And just like that, Synclaire's stomach was heavy again. She squeezed down thoughts of

her math quiz corrections. "I did my vocabulary," she answered carefully.

Her dad played a few notes that sounded like a scale, but a little...off.

"Daddy, do you want me to show you a C scale?" Synclaire asked.

He laughed. "I know I hit a note that doesn't usually belong," said Mr. Fields, "but it had an interesting sound, didn't it? When you were practicing your song just now, I got inspired to improvise a little, like you."

"Improvise?"

"People make a lot of great music by improvising—kind of making it up without planning. And that can lead to something really interesting! Same with what we might call a mistake—lots of musicians end up leaving their mistakes in songs, or get inspired by them to create new songs."

Wow! Synclaire couldn't imagine

Dahhhh duh dah dahhhh dahdahdahdah *PLUNK—*

turning into an actual song. It just sounded WRONG to her. And Synclaire liked doing things right.

That night, Synclaire dreamed she was playing in Carnegie Hall. As she walked onstage and bowed, she smiled at her classmates, who were going wild in the front row. She didn't look toward Mrs. Z, who was all the way up in the back of the balcony. Then she lifted her hands and...

Dahhhh duh dah dahhhh dahdahdahdah *PLUNK—*

The audience was silent. Except for Mrs. Z.

"I'm surprised!" shouted Mrs. Z. "I'm so surprised!"

CHAPTER SIX
OTHER KINDS OF FUN

Mars didn't come by the next morning. Synclaire was quiet as she and Nana walked to school. A few hopeful flakes of snow fell as they walked; maybe this new day would bring good things. Maybe she'd play her song perfectly during her lesson. Synclaire the Piano Kid would dazzle!

When it was time for the Daily Scribble, Synclaire smiled.

The Daily Scribble
for Wednesday, December 18:

What does it mean to be a good friend?

Good friends say kind words to each other, she wrote. *Sometimes they try to make others feel good even when they feel bad.* She thought about helping Fia count her jumps. *Good friends care about each other's activities.* She took out the invitation she'd made for Fia the night before, and added, *I'M SO GLAD WE WILL HANG OUT TOGETHER AFTER SCHOOL!* As far as Synclaire was concerned, this was writing, so it counted as part of her Daily Scribble. Mrs. Z could just be surprised about that, too.

"Let's talk pie," said Mrs. Z at number exploration time. "As in dividing up pieces."

Synclaire scrunched down in her seat.

"Now, if we divide our pie into eight slices—"

"How big are the slices?" asked Thunder.

"What kind of pie?" asked Carlota. "Because it could be a pizza pie."

"If we divide our pie into eight slices," repeated Mrs. Z in her *I'm speaking* voice, "and we give out five slices, what fraction of the pie have we given out?"

Every head in the classroom turned to look at Synclaire.

*Four slices was half of the pie, then five slices was more...but...*What if this was a trick question? Five-eighths? Maybe it had a special name, like fifths-eighths?

Maybe she should keep her mouth shut.

Better to be quiet than embarrassed. Synclaire stared at a tiny gray spot on the white ceiling.

"Anyone can give it a try," called Mrs. Z, looking around the room.

Just then, Mars ran in, breathing hard. "Sorry I'm late," he said to Mrs. Z. "But I have my math quiz corrections right here!" He handed his paper to Mrs. Z with a proud flourish.

Mars had been so casual about the quiz that Synclaire had forgotten to ask how he did. She looked at the floor. He'd done the corrections by himself, which meant that he really didn't believe in her anymore.

"Thank you, Mars. Everyone who has corrections to turn in can bring them up on your way to lunch," said Mrs. Z. "Now, would anyone like to answer our pie question?"

Mars looked at the board. "Um, five-eighths?" he said.

"Thank you, Mars!" said Mrs. Z. "You've made quite an entrance."

Synclaire high-fived her friend as he went to his seat, even though her stomach jumped a little.

As more classmates handed in their corrections, Synclaire squirmed. Her crumpled quiz still sat in her backpack. What was the point of doing corrections when you were supposed to get it right the first time?

Mrs. Z stopped Synclaire on her way out. "Maybe we can chat about Math Club today after school?"

She shook her head. "No, thank you, Mrs. Z," she said in a low voice. "Today I'm going ice-skating with my grandmother." Though Nana might be surprised to hear Synclaire speak as though she was skating, too.

"Ah, got it," said Mrs. Z. "Tomorrow?"

"Um, tomorrow...I—I—," said Synclaire. Just then, Fia returned to the classroom. "Hi, Fia!" she said in a loud voice. "I'm really excited about hanging out today!"

"Me too," said Fia, smiling. "It'll be fun to help your family in the store."

Synclaire avoided Mrs. Z's eyes and followed Fia to the cafeteria.

Synclaire, Mars, and Fia were swapping lunch items when Olive came over. "Thanks for the help with my uncle's hat, Synclaire," she said. "The Math Kid strikes again!"

Synclaire shrugged. "I didn't do any math. I just said to increase the number of stitches for your uncle's head."

"But once you gave me the strategy, I was able to figure it out," said Olive. "Now I can knit other hat patterns in different sizes!" She grinned. "I have something to show *you* that I know you'll like." Olive pulled out a box. "It's one of my favorite board games. It's called Shut the Box and it's very mathy. We can play together sometime."

"I thought you were a Craft Kid, Olive," said Synclaire, eyeing the box.

"I am!" said Olive. "And I love board games, too."

"This looks like fun," said Mars, looking at Shut the Box. "She's right, Synclaire. You roll the dice and add up numbers—you'll love it."

"Well...I'm a Piano Kid now," said Synclaire, wiggling her fingers in a very serious way. "On Friday in music class, I'm going to play a new song called *Snowflake*. Really fast, too, because real piano kids play fast."

"Cool," said Olive. "My grandma says math

and music go together, so I know you'll be really good."

Synclaire wished everyone would stop talking about math. "I've left the numbers game behind," she said. She'd seen someone say that in a movie her parents had been watching.

Kids crowded around their table to watch as Olive, Theo, Poppy, and Mars started a game of Shut the Box right away.

Synclaire focused on carefully opening her yogurt container, pretending not to listen to her classmates laugh and enjoy mathy things as though she wasn't there.

CHAPTER SEVEN
NOT BAD, JUST DIFFERENT

On the way home after school, it seemed like Nana wanted to play a game, too—her own version of Twenty Questions. Thankfully, Fia didn't seem to mind Nana's nosy questions about her WHOLE LIFE and whether she knew each of Nana's Caribbean friends that she "used to run with back in the day." She held Nana's other hand and chatted back with a smile.

Synclaire and Mars showed Fia the different sections in the store.

"That's pretty," said Fia, pointing to the chips display they'd made the day before.

Synclaire noticed that a lot of bags were gone from the top shelf. "Did people buy that many bags already?" she asked her father, who nodded. "Wow!"

"That's what I'm saying," said her father. "I put in another order already, for twice as many, based on how much we've sold."

"Maybe we should display these chips on a lower shelf so that the customers can get them faster," she said slowly.

"That's an excellent idea, my pretty problem-solving pickle," said her father. "I like the way you think."

The kids giggled. They made up a song as they arranged a display of cans. *This is even*

more fun than Beat the Cash Register! thought Synclaire.

"I have another idea," whispered Fia after her mother arrived and settled into a boring grown-up chat with Synclaire's parents. "Since these chips are so popular, I'm going to ask my mom if we can get some now!"

The kids giggled again, and by the time Fia and her mother left the store, the trio had already shared a bag.

Dahhhh duh dah dahhhh dahdahdahdah PLUNK—

Synclaire's piano lesson did not go well at all.

"You seem a bit distracted," said Mrs. Dwyer gently. "Is everything okay?"

"I practiced! I really did, a lot!" said Synclaire.

"I'm sure you did," said Mrs. Dwyer. "You always do."

"Then I don't understand why I keep messing up the song," said Synclaire. Piano Kids did not make so many mistakes!

Mrs. Dwyer packed her red tote bag that said LIFE IS A SONG in elegant black letters. She shrugged. "*Snowflake* is a complicated piece. And some days are just like this," she said. "Mistakes happen to us all."

Synclaire thought about the quiz crumpled up in the bottom of her backpack. She'd already announced to everyone that she was going to play *Snowflake* in music class! She *had* to be perfect.

"Is it true that people who are good at math make good musicians?" she asked, not looking at Mrs. Dwyer. "What about people who are good at other things?"

"I think the most important thing is loving music," said Mrs. Dwyer. "And knowing the way to Carnegie Hall—remember how to get there?"

Synclaire nodded slowly. "Practice, practice." *I did practice! And I'm not perfect. What's wrong with me?*

Mrs. Dwyer nodded. "So why don't we stay with this piece a little longer? It just might need a bit more time. Keep practicing it for next week."

After Mrs. Dwyer left, Synclaire stayed at the piano while Nana got her skating clothes on. She didn't look at her sheet music; she just played.

Dahhhh duh dah dahhhh dahdahdahdah PLUNK—

PLUNK—

Dahhhh duh dah *PLUNK* **dahhhh dahdahdahdah**

Hmmmm. It...didn't sound *bad*. Just...different. Synclaire kept going. She had played the same wrong note so many times that it was starting to sound a little bit right.

CHAPTER EIGHT
WHAT IF YOU FALL?

For someone who was supposed to be skatercizing, Nana was doing a lot of gossiping with her friends as they glided and crisscrossed the ice. The *swish!* of the blades as they went around the rink helped Synclaire think about other things besides the old quiz in her bag and the new math homework sheet they'd gotten that day.

Sort of.

Synclaire had *never* not done her homework. Emma at school had told everyone about No

Homework Day coming up in March. Synclaire wasn't sure how her parents would feel about No Homework Day, even if everyone else was doing it. "Just because everyone else is doing it doesn't make it right," they would say, and Nana would purse her lips and nod in agreement.

Synclaire *did* know how her family would feel about her not doing her homework *today*, and that made her stomach do a backflip. She watched a little girl twirl in the center of the rink, faster and faster until she fell with a hard thump. Ouch. That was embarrassing. Synclaire looked around to see if anyone else had noticed, but no one seemed to be paying attention. She waited for the girl to cry, or yell, or something, but she just sat there.

"Her butt must be getting cold, huh?" said a voice over her shoulder. Synclaire looked up; it was a teenager, so she was automatically cool, but this teenager smiled in a friendly way. She was wearing a red leather jacket over a yellow hoodie and a big, fluffy, knitted scarf. "Don't you come into Doomscroll Comics sometimes? With another kid? My friend Carla works there, and I think I've seen you before."

Wow! A big kid had noticed her. Synclaire nodded. "With my friend Mars. He gets a *SuperMegaFrightFest* comic every week. He says it has clues for how to play the video game, but he still hasn't made it to the highest level."

"Oooh, I love *SuperMegaFrightFest*!" said the girl. "I'm terrible at it. But it's a fun game."

"That's what Mars keeps saying," said Synclaire. "I've never tried, though. I'm pretty sure I'd lose fast."

The girl shrugged. "Okay. So you just play again or whatever. I'm Destiny, by the way." She held out a hand.

"Nice to meet you, Destiny. I'm Synclaire. Synclaire Fields." Saying her full name like that helped her sit up a little straighter.

"My auntie's out there getting her skate on," Destiny said, pointing to an elder wobbling on the ice.

"Nana is, too," Synclaire replied, wondering if she should have said "My grandmother" instead. It was hard enough to remember to say *Mom* and *Dad*!

"Your nana's pretty good," said Destiny as they watched Nana squiggle backward. "I'm going to skate when their class is done. Do you want to come with me?"

Synclaire's eyes widened. Skating with Destiny would be really cool! But what if she fell? Synclaire watched Nana and her friends doing high knees on the ice and giggling. "I like it, but it's embarrassing because I'm always so wobbly," said Synclaire. The little girl was twirling again, a little slower now.

"I'm wobbly sometimes, and I've been skating since I was younger than you," Destiny said. "When I was your age, I thought I'd be an Olympic figure skater. I practiced before school, after school, and after dinner!" She pointed to the ice. "Welp, they're done. I'm going to hit the ice."

"I...I think I will, too," Synclaire said. She wanted to keep hanging out with Destiny.

Destiny introduced herself to Nana, who raised her eyebrows when Synclaire explained that she wanted to get on the ice. But she just helped Synclaire rent some skates and told them to have fun.

A tentative Synclaire tried not to grip Destiny's hand too tightly. "If you're training

for the Olympics, you're probably used to going really fast right away," she said.

Destiny shrugged. "Take your time! We're not in a race. And anyway, I *was* training. But then I got hurt, and the doctor said it wouldn't be good for me to do jumps anymore."

Synclaire's mouth dropped open as she let go of Destiny's hand. "Oh no! I'm sorry! Does it still hurt? Are you okay? Should we stop?"

Destiny laughed. "Thanks for the sympathy. I *was* sad for a little while, but then I realized that the doctor didn't say I couldn't skate *at all*. So now I just have fun being on the ice—*and* I don't have to practice as much!" She held out her arms. "Come on, I'll help you skate backward."

Synclaire focused so hard on wiggling and squiggling backward that she forgot to be embarrassed. When she looked up, she was disappointed to see that they hadn't moved very far. Slowly, she pulled her hands out of Destiny's. "Um, I'm okay if you want to... Whoa!" She wobbled and fell—*PLUNK!*—on the ice.

Destiny pulled her up as a pounding beat blared from the rink loudspeakers. "Come on, let's keep going!"

"Wobble, baby, wobble!" went the song. For a second, Synclaire wondered if the DJ had put the popular party song on because of her tumble, but then Nana skated up to them, saying, "This is my jam!" And Synclaire forgot about falling as all three of them did a very giggly, wiggly, wobbly line dance on the ice.

Back at home, Synclaire ran to the piano before her shower.

Dahhhh duh dah dahhhh dahdahdahdah *PLUNK—*

PLUNK—

Dahhhh duh dah *PLUNK* dahhhh dahdahdahdah

dah dah PLUNK PLINK PLONK dahhhhhhhhh

Dahhhh duh dah dahhhh dahdahdahdah *PLUNK—*

She thought about dancing with Nana and Destiny on the ice as she made up her own song. Improvising was fun! She'd call this song *Fancy Dancy*. Too bad it wasn't complicated enough to play for music class. If she wanted to impress everyone, she'd have to play *Snowflake*. She'd practice it in the morning before school, so it would be fresh.

"Get ready for bed, sweetie pie," said her mother. "Even though you are entertaining us all with your little lullaby."

That night, Synclaire had what Nana called "a good sleep."

CHAPTER NINE
SNOWFLAKES AND SILLY SONGS

Synclaire woke up the next day to the smell of nutmeg, cinnamon, and coconut milk—Momma's porridge! And there was snow outside—not a dusting, but real snow! She got dressed fast and ran downstairs. Maybe if it fell fast enough—like twelve inches per hour—they wouldn't have school!

"Isn't it beautiful?" said Synclaire to her

father, who was wiping his boots on the mat just inside the front door.

He grinned. "It is, superstar, but don't get your hopes up. I don't think this is enough snow for a day off." He turned on the local news radio station, and the family sat around the breakfast table to listen while they dug into their porridge.

Six minutes later, the newscaster said, *"And Curiosity Academy is OPEN today!"* Synclaire groaned, but Nana shushed her because there was more. *"With a one-hour delay!"*

Synclaire cheered just as the doorbell rang. Mars! He must have missed the newscast.

Since they had a little extra time, and a lot of extra porridge, Mars joined them at the table.

"I'm going to open up the store," said Mr. Fields. "See you later, Galloping Gators!"

"What does that mean?" asked Mars.

Synclaire shrugged. "That's how Daddy has fun. Saying things that don't really make sense."

They looked at each other and said *Parents* with their eyes.

"I'm going to walk you two to school today," said Momma. "I'm looking forward to a snowy stroll!"

"I'm a little sore from skatercize," explained Nana. "And I have to be careful about slipping outside."

Synclaire hugged her grandmother. "I'm sorry you can't enjoy a snow walk with us!" she said.

"Oh, I'll enjoy sitting in the living room and watching the flakes fall," said Nana. "With a—"

"Nice cup of tea!" everyone else said with her, and they laughed.

When it was time to leave for school, Synclaire realized that she hadn't practiced *Snowflake* to share with the class! She hoped she was ready to shine. Maybe the real snowflakes would bring her good luck.

As Synclaire and Mars bundled into their coats, hats, scarves, gloves, and boots, she took three little breaths before she made a confession. "I, uh, I was really hoping for a snow day."

"Yeah, that would've been fun."

"For fun reasons, but also...also because I...didn't do my math worksheet," said Synclaire, looking down. "Or my quiz corrections."

Mars stopped. "Why not? Do you want to do them now? I bet we can be a little bit late."

Synclaire shook her head. "No...no, I just... don't like math anymore. Anyway, I got two wrong, remember? It might take a long time if I try to do it now."

"It's a telling-time worksheet! *You* helped *me* with time stuff, remember? You probably just forgot to write something that was in your head. Sometimes you go really fast when you show me something. Maybe you went too fast on your quiz."

"Yeah, and you don't even want my help now that I got two wrong," said Synclaire as Mrs. Fields joined them.

Let's finish this conversation later, Mars said with his eyes.

I don't really want to talk about this but you're my friend so I will, Synclaire's eyes said back.

"I'm excited to hear you play piano in music today," said Mars, giving her a fist bump. "I bet you're going to be amazing!"

Good friends care about each other's activities. "I was thinking," she said out loud, "I wouldn't mind trying *SuperMegaFrightFest* one day, if you still want to show me how to play."

"YES!! How about right now?" He handed her the game console with an encouraging nod. Synclaire took a deep breath and pressed PLAY.

Womp womp womp went the game. She started again. It *womped* again. It *womped* so many more times that it was like a song—a very silly song. Synclaire started beatboxing with the *womps* and Mars laughed. Then Synclaire was laughing too hard to beatbox, and she *womped* and laughed with Mars all the way to school.

CHAPTER TEN
WOMP WOMP PLUNK

Later that morning, as Mrs. Z's class walked to the music room, Synclaire's stomach started doing little hops. *You can do this*, she told herself.

"Do you think we'll get outside recess?" whispered Fia. "I might get to one hundred jumps today."

"I have a special cheer all ready," said Synclaire, squeezing her friend's hand. "And if we have recess in the gym, we can still get a jump rope." Thinking about cheering for Fia made her stomach stop hopping.

But in the music room, the electronic keyboard looked bigger than usual. Synclaire gulped. She was glad that Sharing Time was at the end of the period.

"Since today is already special," began Mrs. Berry, "let's—"

"Throw snowballs inside!" yelled Thunder.

"Pretend it's National Sno-Cone Day?" asked Emma.

"There is not enough snow for that," said Theo.

"There's not enough snow for this much conversation about the snow," said Mrs. Berry, frowning. "This is music time. But instead of the planned lesson, we are going to have Sharing Time for the whole period!"

Synclaire's mouth dropped open as the class cheered.

"Who wants to go first?" asked Mrs. Berry.

"Synclaire's the Piano Kid—she should go first!" said Mars, pumping his fist.

Synclaire knew he was trying to be a good friend, but what if she made a mistake in front of the whole class? She shook her head slowly. "I'll go second," she said. "Or maybe fifth or ninth."

After Memo sang a song that he said was a famous Cuban tune, Mrs. Berry looked at Synclaire, but she shook her head again.

Next Rohan played the violin ("My violin at home is a little more in tune," he said), and Steven played a slow, sad song on the guitar. After each share, Synclaire shook her head at Mrs. Berry until she was the last to go.

"Yay, Synclaire!" whispered Poppy. Mars and Fia gave her high thumbs-up.

Synclaire sat at the keyboard.

She thought about all her practicing and each tip from Mrs. Dwyer.

She remembered how she'd played her piece perfectly three times in a row the week before, and her whole family had cheered.

She made her back straight and held her hands high.

Dahhhh duh dah dahhhh dahdahdahdah PLONK—

Her hands came crashing down on the wrong notes! And not in an *interesting* way. Out of the corner of her eye, she saw Ruthie cover her ears.

"Can I start again?" she asked Mrs. Berry.

But when she tried again, she PLONKED again! So she played faster and faster, wiggling her fingers and dragging them up and down the keys.

Synclaire played worse

and worse

and worse

until she stood up and ran out of the music room, all the way to the bathroom.

And she cried. She'd messed up in front of her whole class! Even if they didn't know she got two wrong on the math quiz, she would definitely be the Mistake Kid after this.

She was wondering if she could stay in the bathroom forever when the door slowly opened. Fia, Olive, and Poppy walked in.

"Are you okay?" asked Poppy. "Mrs. Berry said we could come to check on you."

"I...had a stomachache," said Synclaire, thinking fast. "But it's over."

"You ran out of the music room so fast," said Fia. "Steven wanted to do a duet with you."

Synclaire frowned. "Why?"

"Why not?" asked Olive.

"But I wasn't even good the way a Piano Kid should be," said Synclaire. "Not even close!"

"I loved hearing all the different ways you played—that was cool," said Fia. "I'm making up a dance for my next acting class. Maybe you could come play a song while I dance!"

"I thought it was acting class, not dancing," said Synclaire with a loud sniff.

"We do lots of things. The teacher said one day we're all going to pretend to be animals from different parts of the world. I'm going to be a tiger."

"Oooh, I'd be a kangaroo," said Olive.

"I'd be a corgi," said Poppy. She barked a

little bark, and they laughed. "Are you sure you're okay?" she asked Synclaire.

Synclaire wasn't sure she was okay, exactly. But she was better. *Much better*, she realized. Her friends were still her friends, even though she was sure her piano playing was worse than they'd made it seem. But they weren't even talking about that. So she decided to focus on the fun things they *were* talking about. "I'd be a dolphin!" she said, adding a squeak.

Recess was outside, and even though Synclaire played with Fia, Poppy, and Olive, she smiled at Mars to let him know that they were still best friends, no matter what. Mars smiled back, because he understood.

At the end of the day, Mars and Synclaire put on their coats, hats, and boots slowly until they were the last ones in the cubbies.

Mars shifted from one foot to the other. "About not wanting your help with math. It's not me. It's my mom," he said, tracing a long, winding crack in the floor with the toe of his boot.

That was even worse! "You told Aunt Caroline I got two wrong?" she said.

"No! I mean, my mom said that I had to learn to do my math homework myself!" Mars said quickly. "She knows you never do it *for* me, but she said you do a lot of advanced shortcuts, so when you show me your strategies, I don't really understand the basics, even though your ways are a lot of fun."

What?!?!?! Synclaire stared at Mars. "Then how come you didn't walk to school with us yesterday? It wasn't because I'm not a Math Kid anymore?"

Mars did a few exaggerated fake coughs. "I

overslept because I had a long Dread Heads gaming session the night before. That, uh, was kind of...unauthorized. I'm sorry I didn't explain that."

"Thanks, Mars. I'm sorry that I didn't ask you about this earlier." She smiled. "Let's see if Nana will take us to the bakery after school today! Maybe Fia can come, too."

"Works for me! Hey, you'll always be a Math Kid. I don't know anyone who loves numbers the way you do," said Mars. "One quiz can't change that. I'm a *SuperMegaFrightFest* Kid no matter how many times I fall to my doom!"

CHAPTER ELEVEN
FINDING JOY

That night, as Nana prepared a pot of chamomile tea to go with Momma's special chocolate crackers, Synclaire's mother told a funny story.

"We used to have a big reunion every year with all the cousins, and aunties, and uncles," Mrs. Fields said. "I was the family baker. One year, I had a special cake recipe ready. I baked and frosted it. I held my masterpiece high so that everyone could oooh and ahh, then I put slices on fancy little plates. Some people were so excited they took two!"

"Sounds delicious," said Synclaire.

"Well, that's exactly what it *wasn't*—delicious!" answered Mrs. Fields, laughing. "As I stood there, so proud of myself, watching everyone take their first bite—"

"Whewwwww!" said Nana, scrunching up her face in memory. "Haven't had anything like that since!"

"I'd mixed up the sugar and the salt!" said Mrs. Fields.

"Oh no!" cried Synclaire. Poppy had told her about a time when her grandmother had done the same thing.

Mrs. Fields nodded. "I was so embarrassed! And my cousin Daryl made fun of me for the rest of the reunion. But after I got over being embarrassed, I studied recipes and read instructions carefully, and I also played around, I—"

"Improvised?" asked Synclaire.

Her mother nodded. "Exactly. And I got new ideas for my own recipes—like chocolate crackers!"

Synclaire stared down at the crackers on her plate. "You mean?!"

"Yep," said her mother. "If I hadn't made a big mistake that day, I might not have ever come up with the idea for this—"

"Dainty Delectable Diamond of a Dessert!" finished Mr. Fields. They all laughed.

Synclaire had more chocolate crackers. And two cups of chamomile tea. Then she went to the piano and played her song, *Fancy Dancy*, just for fun. Maybe tomorrow she'd practice *Snowflake*.

At bedtime, Synclaire closed her eyes and snuggled deep under the covers as Mrs. Fields tucked her in. "Today was like your chocolate crackers, Momma—I mean Mom. I made mistakes, then things turned out pretty good. But sometimes it doesn't happen that way."

Mrs. Fields sat at the edge of the bed. "You know, I'm glad you had fun skating yesterday, but I'm looking forward to having you at the store again tomorrow."

Synclaire opened one eye. "Even if I'm not the Number Onecher Number Cruncher anymore?" She opened her other eye and sat up in bed. "I like hearing you say that you're proud of me. What if there's nothing for you to be proud of me for?"

Her mother kissed her forehead. "Oh, honey, we're not proud of you *because* of anything you do. We're proud because you're *you*, number crunching or not."

"But everyone gets excited when I get the right answers, and when I figure—*used* to figure out math stuff really fast. You even got me that Math Kid shirt!"

"I gave you that shirt because you love math, not because you're perfect at math a hundred percent of the time. You can be a Math Kid even if you never get an answer right. Being a Math Kid, or a Piano Kid, or a...Sewing Kid, anything, is about that thing bringing you joy, helping you connect with others, and maybe giving you a way to help other people."

Mr. Fields appeared in the doorway. "And you can be lots of Kids at once, remember? You can love math, and piano, and skating, and...spaceshipping..."

"That's not a word, Daddy," Synclaire said, giggling.

"It should be!" answered her father, coming in and giving her a hug. "Anyway, what if we call you Supercalifragilisticexpialidocious Synclaire for a while? To celebrate all that you are."

"Or just Synclaire," said her mother. "I think Synclaire covers it. We love and are proud of all of you, and what makes having you at the store so special is that we're spending time together. Maybe we all need to remember that."

As Synclaire drifted off to sleep, she heard her parents whispering in the hallway. "I think 'spaceshipping' should be a word," said her father. "I might have to have a word with someone about that. A *word*, get it?"

CHAPTER TWELVE
MANY MULTIPLES OF SYNCLAIRE

Mrs. Z clapped her hands. "I hear a lot of buzzing this morning. Would anyone like to share thoughts about yesterday's snow?"

Fia raised her hand. "I loved it!" she said. "But it melted quickly."

Olive raised her hand. "Maybe we can make snowflakes and hang them up. Then we'll have them to look at any time."

"That's a wonderful idea," said Mrs. Z. She

looked at the clock. "In fact, that was not part of my plan for today, but why don't we take a few minutes to do that now? I think it will help us all settle into the day to do a little quiet arting."

"'Arting' sounds like—" started Thunder, but she stopped because Mrs. Z's eyebrows got so high that Synclaire thought they might leap off her head.

As everyone went to get paper and supplies for snowflake-making, Mrs. Z waved Synclaire over to the hallway just outside the classroom.

"I'm hoping that you and I can finally have a little chat about Math Club," said Mrs. Z.

Synclaire made a face. "Even though I got two wrong on the quiz?" she said.

Mrs. Z frowned. "You did? You didn't turn in your corrections, did you?"

Synclaire shook her head. "I wasn't supposed to get any wrong! I thought Math Kids had to be perfect. And you didn't wink or smile when you gave back my quiz. On the nine perfect scores before that, you winked and smiled."

Mrs. Z frowned deeper. "I didn't mean—hmmm, I'm sorry, Synclaire, I don't remember. Number exploration is not about right answers. And Math Club is for kids who enjoy numbers, and problem-solving, and being a creative thinker—like you! I hope you'll keep being part of the club, not because you have right answers, but because you take so much joy in math. You have fun, and that helps others relax and learn, too. Mistakes on a quiz don't change that. Everyone makes mistakes."

"But I was about to have ten perfect quizzes in a row. Even *you* said you were surprised!" Synclaire added, and it felt good to finally say that out loud.

"I did?" Mrs. Z made a face. "I don't remember that moment, but I might have been surprised about mistakes on topics that I thought you understood well. Or maybe I was surprised that you'd made a careless error...You know what, I apologize. My *words* were careless, and I should have been more thoughtful. I made a mistake, too—I'm sorry."

Having an adult apologize made Synclaire feel itchy and better at the same time. "I accept your apology, and I apologize, too, for not doing my math homework," she mumbled. "Can I still turn in my corrections?"

"Of course!" said Mrs. Z. "There's always time to fix mistakes. And sometimes mistakes lead to good things. Sometimes they even make things better."

Synclaire thought about composing *Fancy Dancy* on the piano. In a way, mathy mistakes had led to some new good fun in her life!

When she went back into the classroom, Synclaire took the crumpled quiz out of her bag. She smoothed the page and squinted; she'd been writing so fast that day that her handwriting was a little sloppy.

Oh! There! She'd been going so fast that she'd forgotten to copy a number! Instead of adding 15 + 25, she'd added 15 + 5, and that had thrown everything off for the next question, too.

15 + 25 = 40, she wrote slowly. Then for the

next question, *40* out of 50 was *4/5*, not 20 out of 50 = 2/5. She checked her work twice before smoothing out the paper again and taking it up to Mrs. Z. Mrs. Z might have winked, but Synclaire wasn't sure. She didn't need it anyway. She smiled and whispered, "Nice work!" to herself.

There were a few minutes of snowflake-making time left. Synclaire showed Poppy how she could fold her paper twice to make four snowflakes that were the same. And then Olive and Fia made theirs like snowflake chains.

"Maybe we can make more of these in the craft club," said Olive. "And maybe I can figure out how to knit a snowflake, too!"

"Yeah!" said Synclaire. "Let's go to the library at recess and see if we can find books to help!" Then she looked over at Fia. Would Fia want to jump rope outside instead? She was so close to her goal of one hundred jumps.

"Yes, we can make a bunch of them," said Fia. "And maybe next week we can all start learning double Dutch together!"

"Double Dutch seems hard," said Synclaire. "*And* fun." She smiled at her friends. "Kind of like piano. I made up a new song. It's called *Fancy Dancy*. Maybe I'll play it in music next week."

"Are you going to wear something fancy, too?" asked Olive.

"I'm going to wear my Math Kid T-shirt. And my long yellow skirt, and my high-tops," Synclaire answered. "So it'll be *Synclaire Fancy*."

"I think you're gonna look *and* be great!" said Fia.

Synclaire smiled. She might play her piece perfectly, or she might not. She could still be a Piano Kid if she wanted to. She might get a perfect score on her next quiz, or she might be doing corrections again. She was still a Math Kid, too. She and Mars might go to the bakery after school or straight to the store. There were so many possibilities....She closed her eyes. Just how many possibilities *were* there, exactly? Was there a way to figure that out?

"It's snowing again!" yelled Mars.

Synclaire opened her eyes. It would be fun to try.

© Stephan Hudson Photography

About the Author

OLUGBEMISOLA RHUDAY-PERKOVICH is the author of many books for young readers, including *Operation Sisterhood; Makeda Makes a Birthday Treat; Someday Is Now: Clara Luper and the 1958 Oklahoma City Sit-Ins; Two Naomis*, coauthored with Audrey Vernick, which was nominated for an NAACP Image Award; and its sequel, *Naomis Too*. She is also the editor of the We Need Diverse Books anthology *The Hero Next Door*. Olugbemisola spent third grade in Yonkers, New York, where her grandparents grew apples, pears, strawberries, and grapes, and now lives with her family in New York City, where she writes, makes things, and needs to get more sleep.

olugbemisolabooks.com.

About the Illustrator

KAT FAJARDO (they/she) received a Pura Belpré Honor for Illustration for their first graphic novel, *Miss Quinces* (published in Spanish as *Srta. Quinces*). Born and raised in New York City, Kat now lives in Austin, Texas, with their pups, Mac and Roni.

katfajardo.com

THE CREATORS OF THE KIDS IN MRS. Z'S CLASS!

- William Alexander
- Tracey Baptiste
- Martha Brockenbrough
- Karina Yan Glaser
- Mike Jung
- Rajani LaRocca
- Kyle Lukoff
- Kekla Magoon
- Kate Messner
- Olugbemisola Rhuday-Perkovich
- Eliot Schrefer
- Linda Urban

Read on for a preview of Book Seven in the series,

Olive Little Gets Crafty

BY **LINDA URBAN**

WHAMMO!

Olive Little had an idea.

A crafty idea.

And because she had a crafty idea, she absolutely, positively could not sleep.

The crafty idea came when Olive was practicing her recorder. Most of the other kids in Mrs. Z's class had gotten pretty good at their recorders, but when Olive practiced, her recorder sounded like her backyard rooster, Doodles, on an ornery day. Olive was very glad when her ten minutes of practice were over, so she could put her recorder back in the old sock Mrs. Berry had called a "recorder case."

No wonder this recorder sounds so ornery, Olive thought. *If I had to live in an old sock, I'd be ornery, too.*

Which is when—WHAMMO!—Olive Little got her very crafty idea.

What if she made her *own* recorder case? She could make something so much better than a sock. Her case would be colorful! And sparkly! With tassels! Or sequins! She had some sequins left over from making the super-sparkly cowl Ayana wore at the variety show… but where were they?

Olive emptied her desk drawers. She searched through her closet. She crawled under her bed. She found balls of yarn and knots of floss and tubes of glue and the arms and legs of a puppet she hadn't figured out the head for yet, but no sequins. How could she make a special, sparkly, not-like-a-sock recorder case without sequins?

"Sally!" Olive bounded down the crickety-creakety stairs of her old house to the family room, where she knew her grandmother would be. Ever since Olive's uncle Roy had set up a wildlife camera in the woods behind their yard, Sally had spent her evenings working on her quilts and watching the footage of the deer and squirrels and porcupines that wandered past. "Sally! I have a sequin emergency!"

Sally pressed the remote and a fat squirrel froze on the TV screen. "That sounds serious."

"The serious-est!" said Olive. "I am making a special sparkly case for my recorder. Sequins are pretty much life or death."

Sally nodded. "I may have some you can use. We'll look for them tomorrow."

Tomorrow? Olive's crafty idea could not wait until tomorrow!

"It's nearly bedtime," Sally said.

Olive groaned. She was sure she had the earliest bedtime of any third grader in Peppermint Falls. Probably the earliest bedtime of any third grader in the world.

"It's a banana pancake day tomorrow," said Sally. "We can't be late."

Sally was the cook at the Curiosity Academy cafeteria. Sally had to get to school extra-extra early to make sure breakfast was ready for all the kids who wanted it.

And because Sally drove Olive to school in the morning, Olive had to go to school extra-extra early, too.